# Spaghetti with the Yeti

Adam & Charlotte Guillain    Lee Wildish

EGMONT

A boy called George had an excellent plan

To go and discover the Yeti.

He put in his backpack a warm woolly hat,

A map and a tin of spaghetti.

MONSTER APE!
THE YETI

SASQUATCH

ABOMINAB
THE BOARD GA

FROM
SIBERIA

ATLAS

WORLD

- For our very own George, A&C Guillain -

- For Oscar, Grace and Laura, LW -

## EGMONT
*We bring stories to life*

### EGMONT LUCKY COIN

Our story began over a century ago, when seventeen-year-old Egmont Harald Petersen found a coin in the street.

He was on his way to buy a flyswatter, a small hand-operated printing machine that he then set up in his tiny apartment.

The coin brought him such good luck that today Egmont has offices in over 30 countries around the world. And that lucky coin is still kept at the company's head offices in Denmark.

FSC MIX Paper from responsible sources FSC® C018306 www.fsc.org

Egmont is passionate about helping to preserve the world's remaining ancient forests. We only use paper from legal and sustainable forest sources.

This book is made from paper certified by the Forest Stewardship Council® (FSC), an organisation dedicated to promoting responsible management of forest resources. For more information on the FSC, please visit www.fsc.org. To learn more about Egmont's sustainable paper policy, please visit www.egmont.co.uk/ethical.

First published in Great Britain 2013 by Egmont UK Limited The Yellow Building, 1 Nicholas Road, London W11 4AN Text copyright © Adam and Charlotte Guillain 2013 Illustrations copyright © Lee Wildish 2013 The moral rights of the author and illustrator have been asserted

ISBN 978 1 4052 6351 1 (Paperback)
ISBN 978 1 7803 1398 6 (Ebook)

A CIP catalogue record for this title is available from the British Library. www.egmont.co.uk

Slowly, George climbed up a steep mountain path
In search of the mythical beast . . .

When he stumbled straight into a monster
Who was eating a sumptuous feast.

"Hurray!"

shouted George,

"I knew you'd be here.

I'm sure that you must be the Yeti."

The monster stood up with a **furious gaze** . . .

"Are you crazy?
My name is Betty!"

"So sorry, Betty," said George with a smile,
"But I'm taking the Yeti some lunch."

"In that case you'll want to take some of these bones,
For the Yeti likes food with a **crunch!**"

So George climbed on up the steep mountain path
To track down the hideaway brute,

When he stumbled upon a big monster
With a face like a battered old boot.

"Yippee!" shouted George, "I've tracked you down now,
I've been searching so long for the Yeti."

The monster glared down
with the angriest growl...

"How **insulting!**
My **name** is Hetty!"

"So sorry, Hetty," said George with a sigh,
"But I'm taking the Yeti a treat."

"In that case you'll want to take one of these goats . . .

For the Yeti likes food with a **bleat**."

So George trudged on up the steep mountain path,

Dragging the goat by her tail,

When he spotted a shape in the distance

And heard the most bone-chilling wail.

"Hurrah!" shouted George, "At last it IS you. I've been looking so hard for the Yeti."

The monster looked down with a horrible howl...

"Are you bonkers? My name is Netty!"

FISH FOOD

"So sorry, Netty," sighed George, feeling glum,

"But I'm taking the Yeti a snack."

"In that case you'll want to take lobsters and crabs, for the Yeti likes food he can **crack!**"

So George plodded on up the steep mountain path,

The difficult climb made him puff.

Exhausted, he threw himself down on the ground,

"That's it!" he cried, "I've had enough!"

As George sat despondent, his head in his hands,

A shadow fell over that place.

He felt something hairy, a prod in the back,

And then turned and peered up at . . .

...a FACE!

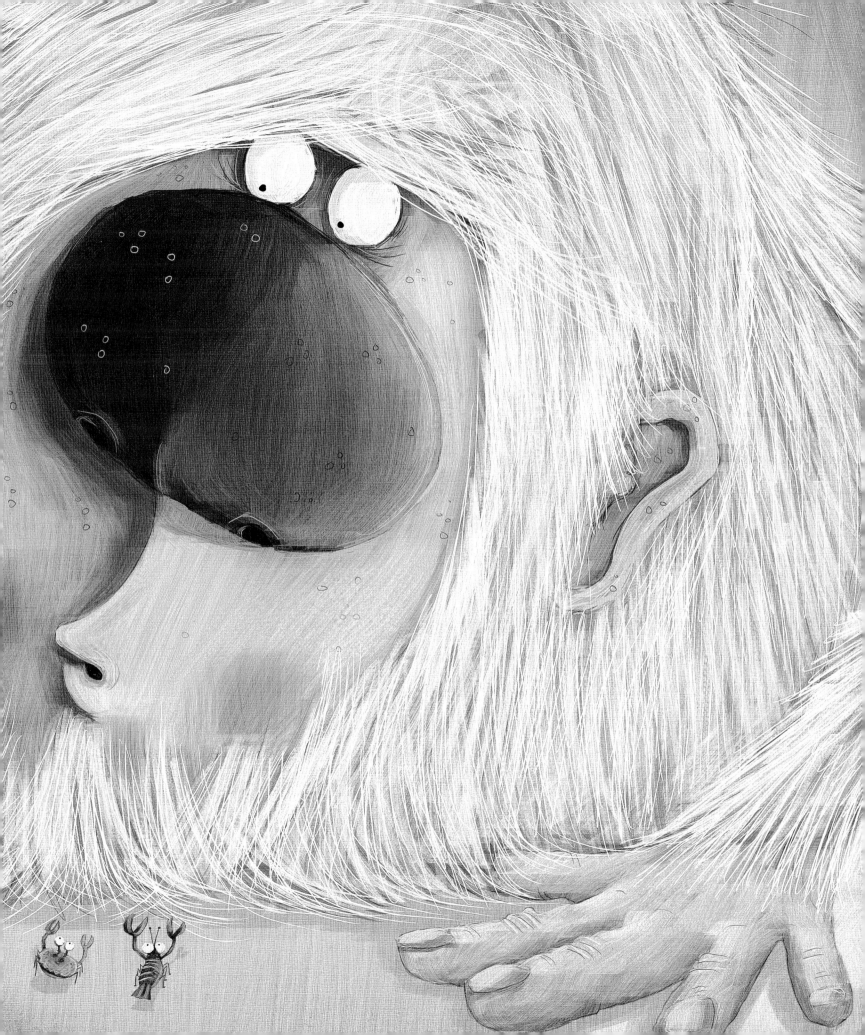

"I've found you!"

cried George, with a big happy grin,

And he showed all his gifts to the Yeti.

But the monster looked down

at the crab and the goat

And said, "Sorry, I just

eat spaghetti."

"I knew it!" said George with a whoop of delight,

And he opened the battered old tin.

Then he tipped the spaghetti out into a bowl . . .

. . . and George and the Yeti tucked in.

SLURP!